Sometimes We Were Brave

Pat Brisson

Illustrated by
France Brassard

BOYDS MILLS PRESS

HONESDALE, PENNSYLVANIA

Our thanks to Commander Scott Calvert, executive officer, Naval Reserve Officer Training Corps, Philadelphia, for his gracious assistance in reviewing the text and illustrations of this book.

Boyds Mills Press, Inc.
815 Church Street
Honesdale, Pennsylvania 18431
Printed in the United States of America

Library of Congress Cataloging-in-Publication Data

Brisson, Pat.
  Sometimes we were brave / Pat Brisson ; illustrated by France Brassard. — 1st ed.
    p. cm.
  Summary: Jerome's mother is a sailor in the United States Navy, and when she is away at sea he tries to be brave even though he misses her and has some bad days.
  ISBN 978-1-59078-586-7 (hardcover : alk. paper)
  [1. Mothers—Fiction. 2. Family life—Fiction. 3. Dogs—Fiction.] I. Brassard, France. II. Title.
  PZ7.B78046So 2010
  [E]—dc22
        2009020251
First edition
The text of this book is set in 14-point Adobe Caslon.
The illustrations are done in watercolor.

10 9 8 7 6 5 4 3 2 1

MY MOM IS A SAILOR.
She works on a big ship.
When her ship is in home port,
she comes home every night.

We bake cookies together.
We read books.
We take our dog, Duffy, for walks.

When her ship goes to sea, she goes, too. She's gone for a long time. Mom hugs me hard before she goes. She hugs Duffy, too. She gives me three kisses in a row. That means "I-Love-You."

She says, "Be brave, Jerome. I'll be back as soon as I can."

I don't feel brave at all. I cry when she leaves. Duffy whines. He gives me lots of sloppy, wet doggy kisses. He licks away my tears.

We miss Mom a lot. I keep her picture next to my bed so I don't forget what she looks like. I show it to Duffy every day so he won't forget, either.

Dad takes good care of us. He doesn't bake cookies like Mom does, but he gives us other good things to eat and reads books to us at night. Duffy likes the books with pictures of dogs in them.

I point to a picture of a dog and ask,
"What does the dog say, Duffy?"
  Woof! Duffy answers. Mom taught Duffy
that trick. It always makes Dad and me laugh.

SOMETIMES WE GET SURPRISES.

My dad gives them to us when he thinks we need them the most. One surprise was a new set of markers and paper to draw on. I decided to make a book for Mom while she's away. Duffy got a squeaky toy that looks like a hot dog. He decided to hide it behind the couch.

SOMETIMES WE HAVE ACCIDENTS.

When Duffy pees on the kitchen floor, he looks so
sorry, I can't be mad at him. "That's okay, Duffy," I tell him.
"I know you didn't mean it." I hold my nose and use a lot of
paper towels to clean it up.

My accidents are in my bed. I hate when that happens.
When I tell Dad, he says, "That's okay, Jerome. That's why
God invented washing machines and bathtubs." Dad says
I'll outgrow it. He says Duffy will, too.

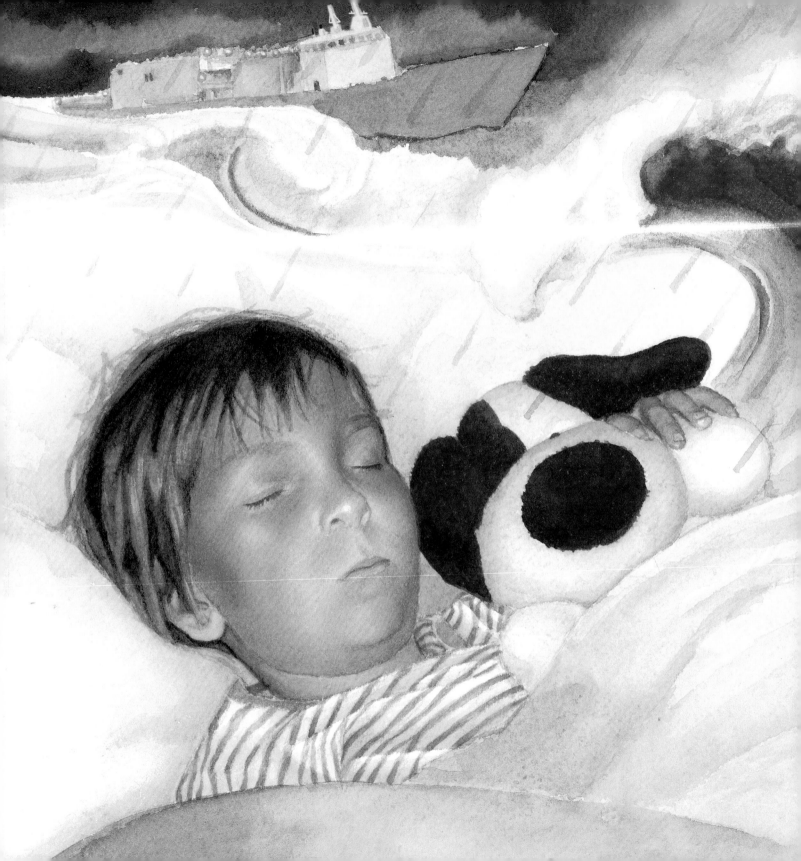

SOMETIMES WE'RE AFRAID.

One night a windy storm knocked over chairs and garbage cans in our backyard. Duffy was so afraid, Dad said we could all sleep in his bed that night, or we'd be too tired to face the morning.

"Is the storm out by Mom's ship, too?" I asked Dad in the dark.

"Can't say for sure, Jerome," he told me. "But if it is, I bet she's lying awake thinking about all of us in this bed and wishing she were here with us, too."

I fell asleep that night picturing Mom on her ship thinking about us and us in Dad's bed thinking about Mom.

SOMETIMES WE GET TREATS.

The day after the storm, we picked up all the branches that had been knocked down. Duffy helped, too, but he thought it was a game and wanted us to throw the sticks so he could fetch them.

When we were done, Dad made ice-cream cones. He made one for Duffy, too, but I had to hold it for him. It dripped all sweet and sticky down my arm. Duffy licked me clean, but Dad made me take a bath anyway.

SOMETIMES WE HAVE BAD DAYS.

The week before my mom was going to come home, I had a really bad day. The kid who sits next to me at lunch spilled his juice all over my pants and then laughed about it. I shoved him hard and his nose hit the table and started to bleed. I was scared, but angry, too. So I pretended to laugh at him. I had to go see the principal, and she called my dad. The other kid went to the nurse.

When I got home, I found out that Duffy had a bad day, too.

He had chewed up one of Dad's favorite sneakers.
We both went to bed early that night. No dessert.
No bedtime stories. Some days are just bad, I guess.
But most of the time we have good days.

The very next day, I took Duffy to a pet show in school. He was so afraid of being around so many other kids and so many other dogs, he hid behind me almost the whole time, except when it was our turn to perform. I was really surprised when my teacher gave him a ribbon for being the bravest.

I said, "Mrs. Paterson, Duffy wasn't brave—he was afraid of everything!"

She smiled at me and scratched Duffy behind his ears. "Jerome," she said, "being brave doesn't mean you're not afraid. Being brave means doing what you're supposed to do *even though* you're afraid. Duffy was afraid of the other dogs and of all the kids. But he didn't run away. He stayed right here and did what he was supposed to—walking, sitting, and shaking hands when you wanted him to. Think about it, okay?"

SOMETIMES WE'RE BRAVE, I GUESS.

Mom asked us to be brave before she left, and I didn't
think we could do it. But Mrs. Paterson said Duffy was brave
at the pet show because he did the things he was supposed
to do. I've been doing the things I was supposed to do, too.
I went to school and took care of Duffy and helped Dad—
even though I was a little bit afraid the whole time, a little bit
afraid about Mom out there on her ship so far from home.
I guess I was being brave after all.

When Mom comes home, I'll give her three kisses in a row and the hardest hug ever. Duffy will give her slobbery doggy kisses, too. Dad will say, "Welcome home, darlin'," and make ice-cream cones for everybody to celebrate.

We'll tell Mom about the night of the storm and show her the ribbon Duffy won at the pet show. I'll give her the book I made for her with my new markers. And I'll tell her that even though we were afraid and worried about her out there on the water so far from home, we did what she asked us to. . . .

We were brave.

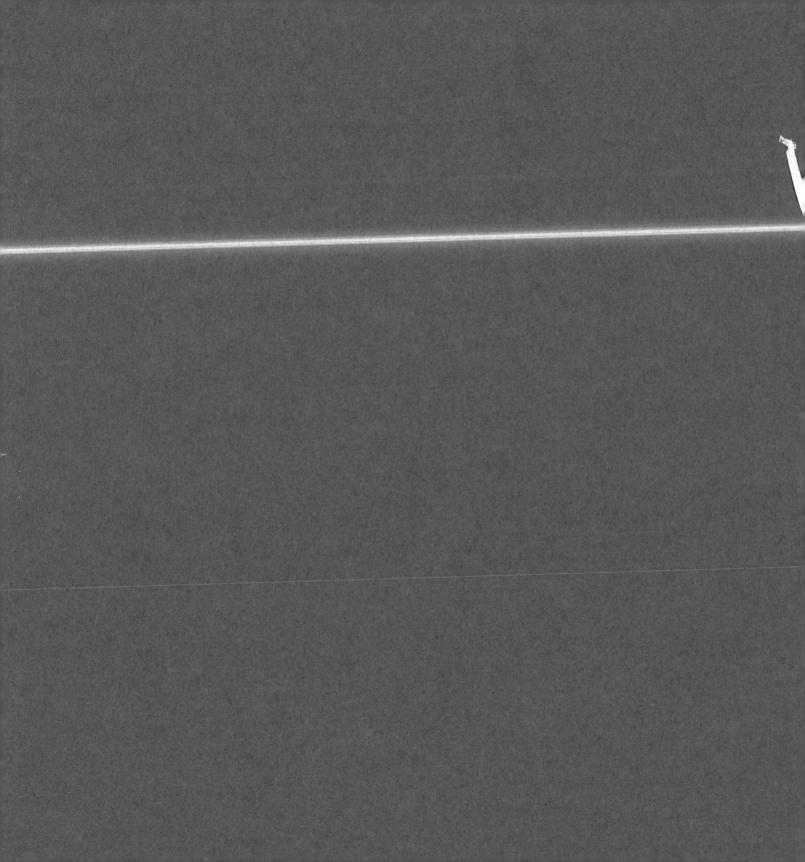